THE THREE KINGS

THE THREE KINGS

A TALE OF FRIENDSHIP, COURAGE, AND VIRTUE

ANTHONY E.

CITIOFBOOKS, INC.
3736 Eubank NE Suite A1
Albuquerque, NM 87111-3579
www.citiofbooks.com
Hotline: 1 (877) 389-2759
Fax: 1 (505) 930-7244

Ordering Information:
Quantity sales. Special discounts are available on quantity purchases by corporations, associations, and others. For details, contact the publisher at the address above.

Printed in the United States of America.

ISBN-13:   Softcover   979-8-89391-441-2
                    eBook   979-8-89391-442-9

Library of Congress Control Number: 2024924386

Table of Contents

CHAPTER 1

The Three Men Who Would Be King

In a land far, far away, there was a kingdom that was ruled by a wise and just king. The king had no heirs, and as he grew older, he knew that he needed to find a successor to take his place. He decided to hold a contest to determine who would be the next king. The rules were simple: three men would be chosen to compete in a series of challenges, and the winner would become the new king.

The first man to enter the contest was Aiden, a brave and ambitious warrior. Aiden had always dreamed of becoming king, and he saw this as his chance to make his dream come true. He was strong and skilled in battle, but he also had a weakness: pride. Aiden believed that he was the best and that no one could defeat him.

The second man to enter the contest was Bael, a cunning and greedy merchant. Bael had always been interested in wealth and power, and he saw this as an opportunity to gain both. He was clever and good at making deals, but he also had a weakness: greed. Bael wanted more than he needed, and he was willing to do whatever it took to get it.

The third man to enter the contest was Corin, a wise and compassionate scholar. Corin had always been interested in knowledge and learning, and he saw this as an opportunity to use his wisdom for the good of the kingdom. He was intelligent and thoughtful, but he also had a weakness: envy. Corin sometimes felt jealous of others who had more than he did.

The three men were very different from each other, but they all wanted the same thing: to become king. They knew that they would have to face many challenges in order to prove themselves worthy of the throne. The kingdom was set in a beautiful landscape with rolling hills and lush green forests. The castle stood tall on top of a hill, overlooking the kingdom below. The people of the kingdom were hardworking and happy, but they were also worried about who would become their next king.

As the contest began, Aiden, Bael, and Corin set out to prove themselves. They faced many challenges, each one testing their strength, intelligence, and courage. But no matter how hard they tried, they couldn't seem to shake their weaknesses.

One day, as they were completing a challenge that involved crossing a narrow bridge over a deep ravine, Aiden's pride got the best of him. He boasted that he could cross the bridge with his eyes closed. But as he tried to do so, he lost his balance and fell into the ravine.

Bael and Corin were shocked by what had happened. They knew that they needed to work together if they were going to complete the challenge and save Aiden. As they worked together to rescue Aiden from the ravine, they realized that they each had something that the other lacked.

Aiden had strength and bravery; Bael had cunning and cleverness; Corin had wisdom and compassion. Together, they were able to overcome their weaknesses and complete the challenge.

As they continued on with the contest, Aiden, Bael, and Corin began to work together more often. They realized that by combining their strengths, they could accomplish much more than they could on their own.

In the end, it was impossible for the king to choose just one of them to be his successor. Instead, he decided that all three men would rule together as co-kings.

And so it was that Aiden, Bael, and Corin became known as the Three Kings of the Kingdom. They ruled with strength, cunning, wisdom, compassion – and just a touch of humor – for many years to come.

CHAPTER 2
The Shaman's Test

After their victory in the first challenge, Aiden, Bael, and Corin continued on their journey to become king. They traveled through the kingdom, facing many challenges along the way. But no matter how hard they tried, they couldn't seem to shake their weaknesses.

One day, as they were traveling through a dense forest, they came across a small hut. Inside the hut lived a shaman, a wise and powerful healer who was known throughout the kingdom for her knowledge and insight.

The shaman invited the three men into her hut and offered them a seat by the fire. She told them that she had been expecting them and that she had a test for them.

The shaman's test was simple: she would ask each man a series of questions to test their knowledge, faith, and integrity. If they answered truthfully and with wisdom, she would reveal their weaknesses to them and tell them how to overcome them.

Aiden was the first to be tested. The shaman asked him about his past, his dreams, and his fears. Aiden answered truthfully, but he struggled with pride. He wanted to be seen as the best and the strongest, even when he wasn't.

The shaman told Aiden that his pride was holding him back. She gave him a talisman – a small stone carved with the symbol of humility – and told him to always keep it with him. She warned him that if he lost it or misused it, his pride would consume him.

Next was Bael's turn. The shaman asked him about his family, his business, and his desires. Bael answered truthfully, but he struggled with greed. He wanted more than he needed and was willing to do whatever it took to get it.

The shaman told Bael that his greed was holding him back. She gave him a talisman – a small coin engraved with the symbol of generosity – and told him to always keep it with him. She warned him that if he lost it or misused it, his greed would consume him. Finally, it was Corin's turn. The shaman asked him about his studies, his beliefs, and his doubts. Corin answered truthfully, but he struggled with sloth. He sometimes lacked the motivation to act and preferred to spend his time in contemplation rather than action.

The shaman told Corin that his sloth was holding him back. She gave him a talisman – a small feather inscribed with the symbol of diligence – and told him to always keep it with him. She warned him that if he lost it or misused it, his sloth would consume him.

With their talismans in hand, Aiden, Bael, and Corin left the shaman's hut and continued their journey. They knew that they still had much to learn and many challenges to face, but they also knew that they had each other – and the shaman's wisdom – to help them along the way. Aiden, Bael, and Corin used their talismans to overcome their weaknesses in different ways.

Aiden, who struggled with pride, used his talisman of humility to remind himself that he was not better than anyone else. Whenever he felt the urge to boast or show off, he would touch the stone and remember the shaman's words. This helped him to stay grounded and focused on what was truly important.

Bael, who struggled with greed, used his talisman of generosity to remind himself that there was more to life than wealth and power. Whenever he felt the urge to hoard or take more than he needed, he would touch the coin and remember the shaman's words. This helped him to be more generous and giving, both with his wealth and with his time.

Corin, who struggled with sloth, used his talisman of diligence to remind himself that action was just as important as contemplation. Whenever he felt the urge to procrastinate or avoid doing something difficult, he would touch the feather and remember the shaman's words. This helped him to be more proactive and motivated, both in his studies and in his actions.

By using their talismans in this way, Aiden, Bael, and Corin were able to overcome their weaknesses and become better versions of themselves. They learned that it was not enough to simply have a talisman – they had to use it actively and consciously to truly benefit from its power.

CHAPTER 3
The Land of Sinking Sand

After leaving the shaman's hut, Aiden, Bael, and Corin continued on their journey to become king. They traveled through many lands, facing many challenges along the way. But their greatest challenge was yet to come.

One day, they arrived at the edge of a vast desert known as the Land of Sinking Sand. The desert was full of dangers and temptations, and many travelers had been lost in its shifting sands.

The three men knew that they had to cross the desert if they were going to continue their journey. But they also knew that it would not be easy. They would have to avoid touching anything that might turn to dust, as well as resist the illusions and mirages that tried to lure them away from their path.

As they entered the desert, Aiden, Bael, and Corin felt the heat of the sun beating down on them. The sand was hot and shifting beneath their feet, making it difficult to walk. But they pressed on, determined to reach the other side.

As they traveled deeper into the desert, they began to see strange things. They saw beautiful oases with cool water and lush greenery, but when they reached out to touch them, they turned to dust. They saw towering cities with glittering towers and bustling markets, but when they tried to enter them, they disappeared.

Aiden, Bael, and Corin knew that these were illusions and mirages, meant to lure them away from their path. They resisted the temptations and continued on their way.

But as they traveled further into the desert, they began to feel the effects of their weaknesses. Aiden's pride made him want to prove himself by taking unnecessary risks. Bael's greed made him want to hoard water and supplies, even though they needed to share them. Corin's sloth made him want to rest and avoid the difficult journey ahead. each man also had his talisman to help him overcome his weakness. Aiden touched his stone of humility and remembered that he was not better than anyone else. Bael touched his coin of generosity and remembered that there was more to life than wealth and power. Corin touched his feather of diligence and remembered that action was just as important as contemplation.

With their talismans in hand, Aiden, Bael, and Corin were able to overcome their weaknesses and continue their journey. They faced many dangers and temptations along the way, but they never lost sight of their goal.

Finally, after many days of travel, they reached the other side of the desert. They were tired and thirsty, but they were also stronger and wiser than before. They had learned valuable lessons about humility, generosity, and diligence – lessons that would serve them well in the challenges ahead. Aiden, Bael, and Corin traveled through many lands on their journey to become king. Some of the other lands they traveled through might have included:

The Forest of Shadows: A dense and dark forest filled with twisted trees and hidden dangers. The three men would have had to use their wits and their skills to navigate through the forest and avoid its many traps and pitfalls.

The Mountains of Mist: A range of towering mountains shrouded in mist and fog. The three men would have had to climb steep cliffs and cross narrow ledges to make their way through the mountains, all while avoiding the treacherous winds and sudden storms that plagued the range.

The River of Dreams: A wide and winding river that flowed through the heart of the kingdom. The three men would have had to build a raft or find a boat to cross the river, all while avoiding the dangerous currents and hidden rocks that lurked beneath the surface.

The Plains of Promise: A vast expanse of rolling grasslands dotted with small villages and farms. The three men would have had to travel across the plains, meeting the people who lived there and learning about their customs and traditions.

Each land presented its own unique challenges and dangers, but Aiden, Bael, and Corin faced them all with courage and determination. They learned much on their journey, both about themselves and about the world around them. As Aiden, Bael, and Corin traveled through the kingdom, they would have encountered many different customs and traditions. Some of the customs and traditions they might have learned about could include:

Festivals and celebrations: The people of the kingdom would have had many festivals and celebrations throughout the year, each one marking a different event or occasion. Aiden, Bael, and Corin might have joined in the festivities, dancing, singing, and feasting with the locals.

Rites of passage: The people of the kingdom would have had many rites of passage to mark important milestones in a person's life. Aiden, Bael, and Corin might have witnessed or participated in these rites, learning about the customs and traditions that were important to the people.

Hospitality and generosity: The people of the kingdom would have been known for their hospitality and generosity. Aiden, Bael, and Corin would have been welcomed into homes and villages along their journey, sharing meals and stories with the locals.

Arts and crafts: The people of the kingdom would have been skilled in many different arts and crafts. Aiden, Bael, and Corin might have seen beautiful paintings, intricate carvings, or finely woven textiles on their journey. Each custom and tradition would have taught Aiden, Bael, and Corin something new about the people of the kingdom and their way of life. By learning about these customs and traditions, they would have gained a deeper understanding of the kingdom they hoped to rule.

CHAPTER 4
The Hilltop of Dreams

After crossing the Land of Sinking Sand, Aiden, Bael, and Corin continued on their journey to become king. They traveled through many lands, facing many challenges along the way. But their greatest challenge was yet to come.

One day, they arrived at the base of a tall hill known as the Hilltop of Dreams. At the top of the hill was a forest full of mushrooms that caused hallucinations and nightmares. The three men knew that they had to enter the forest if they were going to continue on their journey. But they also knew that it would not be easy. They would have to distinguish between reality and fantasy, as well as face their deepest fears and regrets.

As they climbed the hill, Aiden, Bael, and Corin felt a sense of unease. The air grew thick and heavy, and strange sounds echoed through the trees. But they pressed on, determined to reach the top.

When they entered the forest, they were immediately surrounded by a dense fog. The mushrooms grew thick on the ground, releasing their spores into the air. Aiden, Bael, and Corin began to see strange things – visions of their past, present, and future.

Aiden saw visions of his past failures – battles he had lost, friends he had betrayed. He felt a deep sense of shame and regret, but he also knew that he had to face these memories if he was going to move forward.

Bael saw visions of his future losses – wealth that would slip through his fingers, power that would fade away. He felt a deep sense of fear and uncertainty, but he also knew that he had to face these fears if he was going to find true happiness.

Corin saw visions of his present doubts – questions that plagued him, decisions that weighed on him. He felt a deep sense of confusion and indecision, but he also knew that he had to face these doubts if he was going to find clarity.

As they made their way through the forest, Aiden, Bael, and Corin faced their fears and regrets head-on. They used their talismans – Aiden's stone of humility,

Bael's coin of generosity, Corin's feather of diligence – to help them stay grounded in reality.

Finally, after what seemed like an eternity, they emerged from the forest and reached the top of the hill. They were exhausted and shaken, but they were also stronger and wiser than before. They had faced their deepest fears and regrets – and they had emerged victorious.

CHAPTER 5
The Valley of Desire

After leaving the Hilltop of Dreams, Aiden, Bael, and Corin continued on their journey to become king. They traveled through many lands, facing many challenges along the way. But their greatest challenge was yet to come.

One day, they arrived at the edge of a wide valley known as the Valley of Desire. In the center of the valley flowed a river full of seductive creatures and objects that tried to entice travelers with pleasure and power. The three men knew that they had to cross the river if they were going to continue on their journey. But they also knew that it would not be easy. They would have to avoid touching anything that might harm them or corrupt them, as well as resist the urges and impulses that tried to control them.

As they entered the valley, Aiden, Bael, and Corin felt a sense of temptation. The river flowed before them, its waters sparkling in the sun. Strange creatures swam in its depths, beckoning to them with promises of pleasure and power.

But the three men knew that they had to resist these temptations. They began to make their way across the river, using stepping stones and fallen logs to keep their feet dry.

As they crossed the river, they were beset by urges and impulses. Aiden felt a strong desire for lust, his eyes drawn to the seductive creatures that swam in the water. Bael felt a strong desire for gluttony, his stomach rumbling at the sight of the delicious food that floated on the surface. Corin felt a strong desire for envy, his heart filled with jealousy at the sight of the wealth and power that lay within reach.

But each man also had his talisman to help him overcome his weakness. Aiden touched his stone of humility and remembered that true love was more important than fleeting pleasure. Bael touched his coin of generosity and remembered that sharing was more satisfying than hoarding. Corin touched his feather of diligence and remembered that hard work was more rewarding than envy. With their talismans in hand, Aiden, Bael, and Corin were able to resist their urges and impulses and continue on their journey. They faced many temptations along the way, but they never lost sight of their goal.

Finally, after many hours of travel, they reached the other side of the river. They were tired and hungry, but they were also stronger and wiser than before. They had learned valuable lessons about lust, gluttony, and envy – lessons that would serve them well in the challenges ahead. Aiden, Bael, and Corin faced many challenges on their journey to become king. Some of the other challenges they might have faced could include:

The Labyrinth of Lies: A maze of twisting passages and dead ends, filled with traps and illusions. The three men would have had to use their wits and their skills to navigate through the labyrinth and avoid its many dangers.

The Tower of Trials: A tall tower with many levels, each one presenting a different challenge. The three men would have had to climb the tower, facing physical, mental, and emotional trials along the way.

The Pit of Peril: A deep pit filled with dangerous creatures and treacherous terrain. The three men would have had to descend into the pit, using their strength and their courage to overcome the obstacles that lay in their path.

The Bridge of Betrayal: A narrow bridge spanning a wide chasm, with many traps and pitfalls. The three men would have had to cross the bridge, facing the temptation to betray each other in order to gain an advantage.

Each challenge would have tested Aiden, Bael, and Corin in different ways, forcing them to confront their weaknesses and overcome their fears. But through it all, they would have relied on each other – and on their talismans – to help them succeed.

EPILOGUE
The New King

After facing many challenges and overcoming many obstacles, Aiden, Bael, and Corin finally completed their journey. They returned to the shaman's hut, where she evaluated their progress and declared the winner.

The winner was Corin, who had shown the most balance and virtue among the three. He had faced his doubts and fears with courage and wisdom, and he had proven himself to be a worthy successor to the throne.

Aiden and Bael accepted Corin's victory gracefully. They pledged their loyalty to him and vowed to support him in his rule.

Corin was crowned as the new king in a grand ceremony attended by all the people of the kingdom. He vowed to rule with justice and wisdom, using the lessons he had learned on his journey to guide him.

And so it was that Corin became known as the Wise King, ruling over the kingdom with fairness and compassion. Aiden and Bael served as his loyal advisors, using their strength and cunning to help him make the best decisions for the kingdom.

Together, the three men brought peace and prosperity to the land. They faced many challenges along the way, but they always remembered the lessons they had learned on their journey – lessons about humility, generosity, diligence, lust, gluttony, envy, pride, greed, sloth – and they used these lessons to guide them in their rule and so it was that the kingdom flourished under their wise and just leadership – a testament to the power of friendship, courage, and virtue.

THE END